The Charge of the EnteleTrons

The world may have started with a wise, whispered word.
Or it could have begun with the biggest BANG ever heard.

At that moment in time, countless particles would be
The basis of everything, even you, even me.

In that blink of an instant, a group rose from the glow,
with the mission to t-e-a-c-h and to s-h-o-w what they know.

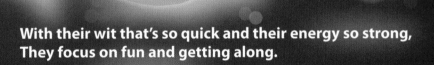

With their wit that's so quick and their energy so strong,
They focus on fun and getting along.

A proton named Priti and a neutron named Ning,
stick together forever and fix everything.

With Ellie the electron, the group is complete,
so the world stays together, correct, and so NEAT.

Some say this group lives in a far, distant place.
But, the truth is *they live through all time and all space.*

Where's Green?

By Renée Heiss and Gary A. Stewart
Illustrated by Fay Cofrancesco

For information about permission to reproduce sections from this book, please visit the Entelechy Education, LLC website at www.entelechyed.com

Library of Congress Cataloging-in-Publication Data
Where's Green? / written by Renée Heiss and Gary A. Stewart; illustrated by Fay Cofrancesco

Summary: *Where's Green?* is part of a children's picture book series for lower elementary readers. The series presents three unique characters (subatomic particles) that set the world right with their questions, exploration, and recommendations.
This book presents the concepts of the colors of the rainbow and cooperation. The accompanying *EnteleKey™* Learning Guide explores alliteration.

ISBN# 978-0-9887813-0-6

Library of Congress Control Number: 2012955993

First Edition

Printed in the United States of America

One night, The EnteleTrons bounced around the forest.
They looked for a new adventure.

Soon the sun came up. It cast shimmering shadows on the morning dew.

Suddenly, the team stopped bouncing. "Look!" said Priti.
"The pine trees are all brown. And the oak trees are brown, too." Green was gone.

"What's going on?" asked Ellie.

"This is a mystery," said Priti.

"Let's find out what happened," suggested Ning.

"Maybe the green fell off," Ellie suggested. She went to a tall tree.
She looked under the little leaves. She did not find green anywhere.

"Don't be silly, Ellie," said Priti. "Colors don't fall off of trees. Sunlight sends all the colors to earth. Some things hold all the colors. They are white. Other things let one color free. That's the color we see."

Zip, Zap, Zingle!
Ning whooshed to the EnteleLab
where the EnteleTrons keep all their
scientific instruments.
He knew what would help Ellie understand.

Look on page 24 to see if you can figure out what Ning will bring.

Ning held up a prism. Beautiful colors formed a rainbow.

But one color was missing.

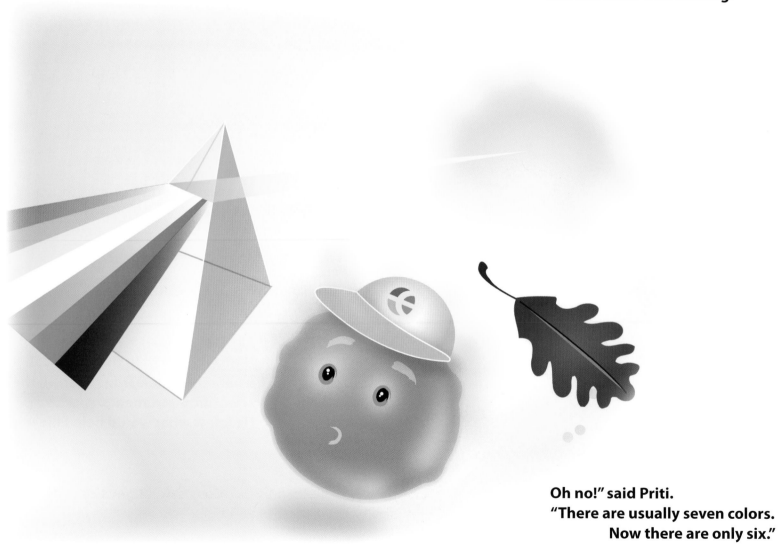

Oh no!" said Priti.
"There are usually seven colors.
Now there are only six."

Ellie made sure they didn't miss any other colors. "There are Red and Orange.
Next to them are Yellow and Blue. Now I see Indigo and Violet.
There's no Green anywhere. Something happened to Green.
I hope Green isn't sick."

"Don't be silly, Ellie," said Priti. "Colors don't get sick.
Colors don't fall and colors don't get sick."

"Then where is all the green? Maybe the trees just need water.
Maybe they're all dried out," suggested Ning. Just then, dark clouds swirled above the faded forest.

Rain poured down. It soaked the ground.

The rain didn't make any difference.
The trees were still brown.

The grass was still brown.
Ning looked around.

Then he found a clue in the sparkling sky.

7

A rainbow arched above them. Again, only six colors formed the rainbow.
A huge hole ran through the middle. That was where Green should have been.

"Come on," suggested Ning.
"Let's go see if the rainbow knows what happened to Green."

"Ning, how will we find our way back from the rainbow?" Priti asked.

**Zip, Zap, Zingle!
Ning whooshed to the lab.**

*Look on page 24 to see if you can
figure out what Ning will bring.*

9

When Ning returned, he held a magic map and a compass.
He followed the path to the rainbow, so he knew how to get back.

"Great idea," Ellie said.

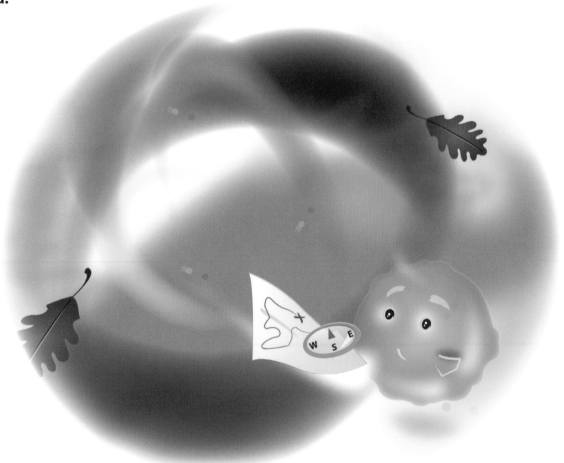

Soon, The EnteleTrons arrived at the rainbow. They found jumbled colors.
Yellow and Blue were arguing. Red just barely held on to Orange.
Indigo and Violet were trying to pull the group together.

"This is not good," said Ellie. "We will never get Green back now."

"We have to think of something fast," said Priti.
She twirled the prism around and around.

Ning put the map and compass into his pocket. Then he pulled out a white whistle.
He blew as loudly as he could. He wanted to get their attention. It worked!

All the rainbow colors stopped their bickering. They stared at Ning.

"What happened to Green?" Priti asked. It was the wrong question to ask.

They all shouted at once. Each color tried to be the loudest to tell its story.

Ning whistled again. He tried a different way to quiet the rainbow.

"I am going to give this prism to one color. Only that color will tell its story.
When you are done, please hand it back to me. Swirl your colors if you agree."

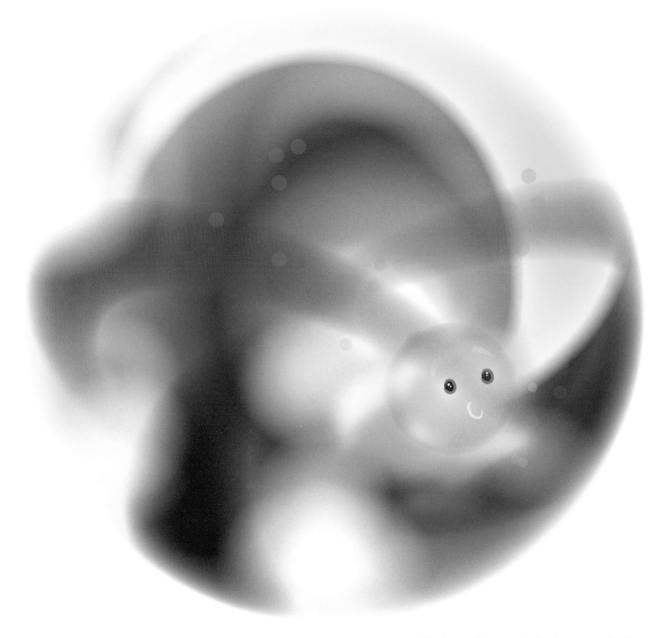

All the colors swirled around Ellie.

She felt like she was in the middle of a twirling tornado!

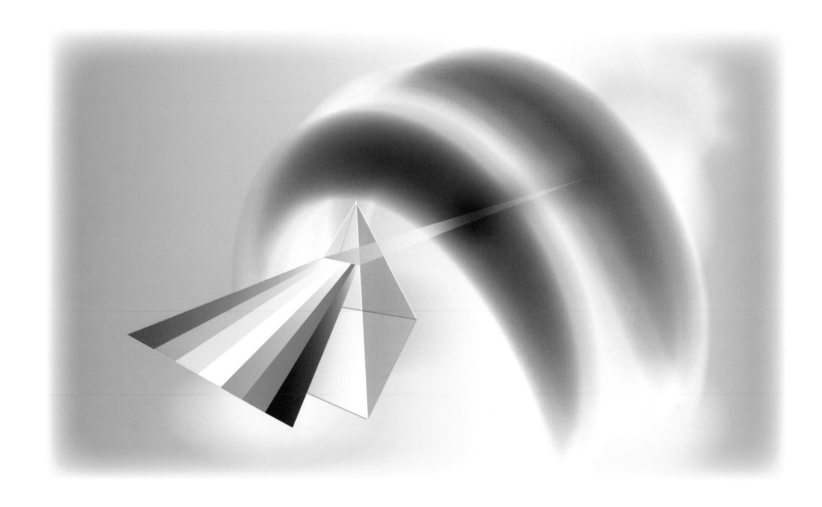

Then Ning whistled again. The rainbow went back into place. Green was still missing.

Ning held up the prism. He said, "I am going to give this prism to the primary colors.
Red, you will be first. Yellow will be second. Blue will speak third."

Red said, "It all started when we decided to change places. We were tired of the same old order. Then one thing led to another. Green simply left the group. It got tired of all the bickering."

Ning took back the prism.
"You can't get all mixed up. Everyone will become confused. This is all wrong!"

Priti took the prism from Ning.
"We don't have any green trees in the forest. Summer looks like a very dull, dry autumn."

Priti gave the prism to Yellow.
"I'm afraid I may have started this. I told Green that it couldn't be
between me and Blue anymore."

Blue jiggled and wiggled. Blue wanted to hold the prism.
Ning took the prism from Yellow. Then he gave it to Blue.

"No, it's really my fault," added Blue. "It was my idea to mix up the colors. I wanted to be at the top of the rainbow. I'm sorry. I miss Green."

Ellie thought she saw rainbow tears dripping from the rainbow.

Suddenly, Green whooshed back into place.

"Green!" all the colors shouted.

"Welcome back, Green," said Ellie. "We are so glad you returned. I didn't really believe you were sick!"

"But I was sick," Green explained.
"Sick of all the arguing. I'm glad the rainbow likes its order again."

So Green went back in place between Yellow and Blue.

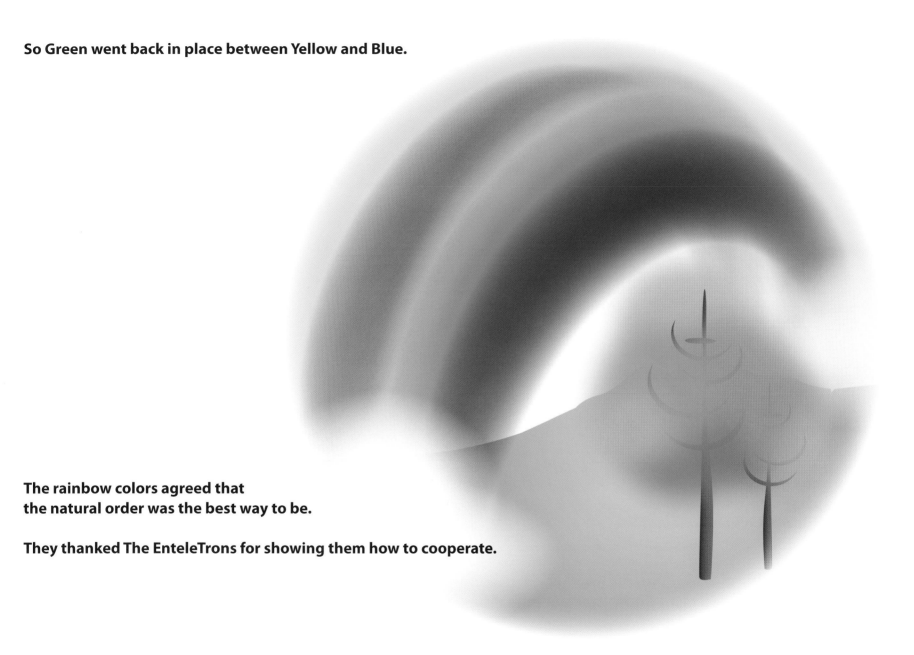

The rainbow colors agreed that
the natural order was the best way to be.

They thanked The EnteleTrons for showing them how to cooperate.

They learned how to do their jobs within the group.

The EnteleTrons looked around. So many colors surrounded them.
A curtain of rain fell. The rainbow shone in the blue sky.

"This is good," Ning declared. "The rainbow is complete again."

"Wait. I don't get it," said Ellie.
"Why do we see the rainbow when
the sky is blue but it's also raining?"

"Because," Priti the proton explained, "you need water in the sky to see a rainbow.
That acts like a prism. Sunlight goes through the water. That forms the rainbow we see.
Everything must work together to create the rainbow."

That made Ellie the electron very happy. She liked to make connections.

Finally, after all the confusion,
the universe returned to its natural order, thanks to The EnteleTrons.

The EnteleTrons return to their EnteleLab frequently to use the tools on their shelves to solve mysteries and help the universe return to its natural order.

See if you can figure out which tools they will use on pages 3 and 9.

Glossary and link to website activities

PRISM – a pyramid-shaped crystal that separates sunlight into seven colors.

COMPASS – a device that shows north, south, east, and west. It contains a magnet that aligns the needle with earth's magnetic north pole.

For fun related activities, go to http://www.entelechyed.com/entelekids

For extended learning activities, go to http://www.entelechyed.com/entelekey__learning_guides

The entire universe is made up of billions of atoms. Everything has teeny tiny atoms that combine into molecules. The molecules combine to form everything you see around you. Everything! Those molecules could be as simple as water. It has an atom of oxygen and two atoms of hydrogen in every molecule. Other molecules have many atoms working together. They make everything from the sun to your favorite ice cream. So when you read about The EnteleTrons™ and their adventures, think about how tiny they are in size, but how huge they are in their effect on the universe. You can be just like The EnteleTrons. Think about how you can make a huge difference in other people's lives, too.

Entelechy
Education, LLC

Have a *Where's Green?* Party

NUMBER OF PLAYERS

6 (or six teams)

PREPARATION

Write the name of each color of the rainbow on separate index cards: RED, ORANGE, YELLOW, GREEN, BLUE, INDIGO, and VIOLET.

HOW TO PLAY

Ask someone who is not playing the game to hide the card labeled GREEN. Everybody else gets a card with a color name on it. The object of the game is to find GREEN. When each player finds the GREEN card, he secretly places his card with GREEN. That person then helps one other person to find GREEN by providing verbal clues. No pointing is allowed! When everyone has placed his or her card, retrieve the pile of cards and arrange in rainbow order.

NOTE

There are no winners or losers in this game, only cooperative play to achieve a common goal.

AFTER THE GAME

You can hide GREEN in a different location and play again. Or you can have green refreshments: Green JELL-O, green juice, green salad, green cupcakes, etc. While you eat, talk about what would happen if you didn't have anything green in the world.

Entelechy
Education, LLC

ABOUT THE **Authors** and **Illustrator**

Renée Heiss, *Co-Author*

As a founder of Entelechy Education, LLC and co-author of The EnteleTrons™ series, Renée Heiss is an award-winning children's author and retired teacher of child development. She was the 1997 New Jersey Family Consumer Sciences Teacher of the Year. In 2008, she was honored as a Baldwin fellow at the University of Wisconsin at Madison for a Nanotechnology Meets Biotechnology conference. She is an instructor for the Institute of Children's Literature and a member of the Society of Children's Book Writers and Illustrators.

Gary A. Stewart, *Co-Author*

As a founder of Entelechy Education, LLC and co-author of The EnteleTrons™ series, Gary A. Stewart has a unique record of accomplishment in the areas of strategic planning, domestic and global business development, marketing and sales, and operational management. Gary has been actively involved in all major facets of the pharmaceutical industry, leveraging his scientific and business background to promote entrepreneurship, strategic and critical thinking, innovation and creativity. Gary is a successful inventor and active educator.

Fay Cofrancesco, *Illustrator*

As illustrator of *Where's Green?* and the original EnteleTrons™ characters, Fay Cofrancesco runs her own design and illustration firm: Fluid Marketing, in Maryland. A native of upstate NY, Fay transferred to Baltimore in 2003 on a scholarship, completing her BFA in Illustration from Maryland Institute College of Art in 2005, and later completing her MBA in 2011. Fay's experience ranges from natural science illustration, to print, publishing, and electronic media production in various industries.

Entelechy
Education, LLC